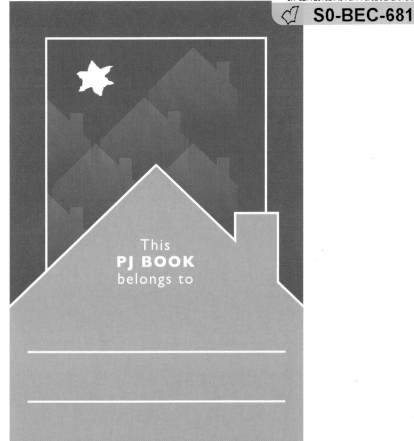

This
PJ BOOK
belongs to

_____

_____

JEWISH BEDTIME STORIES and SONGS

To Steven—
our very own Papa,
who makes the best blackened latkes

SQUARE
FISH

An Imprint of Macmillan
175 Fifth Avenue
New York, NY 10010
mackids.com

Square Fish and the Square Fish logo are trademarks of Macmillan and
are used by Henry Holt and Company under license from Macmillan.

Square Fish books may be purchased for business or promotional use. For information on bulk
purchases, please contact the Macmillan Corporate and Premium Sales Department at
(800) 221-7945 x5442 or by e-mail at specialmarkets@macmillan.com.

Library of Congress Cataloging-in-Publication Data
Zalben, Jane Breskin.
Papa's latkes: story and pictures by Jane Breskin Zalben.
Summary: Papa and the little bears make latkes for Chanukah. Includes the song
"O Chanukah" and a recipe for making latkes.
[1. Chanukah—Fiction. 2. Cookery—Fiction. 3. Jews—Fiction. 4. Bears—Fiction.]
I. Title. PZ7.Z254 Pap 1993   E—dc20   93-37986
ISBN 978-1-250-04668-0

Originally published in the United States by Henry Holt and Company
First Square Fish Edition: 2013
Typography by Jane Breskin Zalben.
The text type was set in Caslon 540.
The art was done with a 000 brush using watercolors on imported Italian paper.
Square Fish logo designed by Filomena Tuosto

10 9 8 7 6 5 4 3 2 1

PAPA'S LATKES

STORY AND PICTURES BY
Jane Breskin Zalben

SQUARE
FISH

HENRY HOLT AND COMPANY
New York

Mama made the best
potato pancakes in the whole town.
"This Chanukah," she said, "I don't
feel like making latkes." So Papa
said, "Let's have a latke contest!"
Beni flipped his latke in the air.
And it landed on Sara's head.

Rosie added extra potatoes.
Her latkes were lumpy.

Max's were so oily, they slipped
right off the plate into Leo.

Leo made his into strange shapes.

No one would eat them.

Blossom's were too brown.
Goldie's were too raw.

Molly's were too large.
Sam's were too small.

Finally, Papa cried, "Step aside."
He peeled and grated and mixed the
potatoes until the batter was smooth.
Everyone watched carefully. He made
pancake after pancake after pancake.
They were stacked so high, Papa and
Mama nearly disappeared.

When Papa was done, the whole family
helped carry all the latkes to the table.
Mama put a dab of fresh sour cream and
homemade applesauce next to each one.
They weren't too dark.
They weren't too light.
All agreed, "These are perfectly round,
and just right. Let's celebrate!"

Candles were lit in the menorah.
Mama's favorite song, "O Chanukah,"
was sung many times. Everyone danced,
played dreidel, and opened presents.

For the first night of Chanukah,
each cousin got a bag of chocolate
gelt, and a new, shiny frying pan.
"To make your own latkes," Papa said,

"for all eight nights."
"But yours are the best!" Beni shouted.
"Yours will be too!" Papa smiled.
"I'll teach you how tomorrow."

Papa gave everyone a kiss. So did Mama. "Now go to sleep," they both whispered. And the children did, with their tummies stuffed with Papa's latkes.

O Chanukah

Arranged by Alexander Zalben

O Cha-nu-kah, O Cha-nu-kah, come light the Me-no-rah.
Oy Cha-nu-koh, oy Cha-nu-koh, a yom-tov a shay-ner, a

Let's all have a par-ty, we'll all dance the ho-rah.
lus-stig-er, a fray-lich-er, nit-du noch a zoi-ner,

Gath-er 'round the ta-ble; you'll get a treat. Shi-ny tops to play with,
al-le nacht in drayd-lech shpie-len mir, zi-dig bay se lat-kes